W9-BRA-668

MAKE WAY FOR DUMB BUNNIES

by Dav Pilkey

THE BLUE SKY PRESS / AN IMPRINT OF SCHOLASTIC INC. NEW YORK

For Kevin Lewis D. P.

THE BLUE SKY PRESS

Library of Congress catalog card number: 95-15311

ISBN-13: 978-0-545-03939-0
ISBN-10: 0-545-03939-8

12 11 10 9 8 7 6 5 4 3 2 07 08 09 10 11

Printed in Singapore 46

This edition first printing, September 2007

The illustrations in this book were done with watercolors, India ink, acrylics, gouache, skim milk, and Vick's Vap-O-Rub.

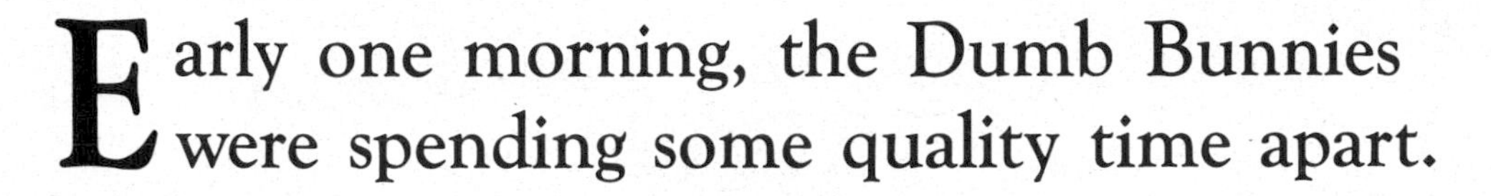

Early one morning, the Dumb Bunnies were spending some quality time apart.

Poppa Bunny was watching the Super Bowl,

Momma Bunny was watching the Orange Bowl...

...and Baby Bunny was watching the Toilet Bowl.
"That's my boy!" said Poppa Bunny.

Soon it started to rain. Dark clouds rolled in, and thunder flashed brightly all around.

"It looks like a *perfect* day to go to the beach," said Poppa Bunny.

So they packed three sack lunches...

…loaded up the car with everything they needed,

and headed off for the beach.

When they got to the beach, the Dumb Bunnies went in for a swim.

Baby Bunny took his umbrella, because he didn't want to get wet.

Afterwards, Momma Bunny combed the beach,

Poppa Bunny went fishing in a boat…

...and Baby Bunny blew up an inflatable raft.

"That's my boy!" said Poppa Bunny.

Soon the rain stopped, and the sun came out.
"Looks like bad weather," said Momma Bunny.
So the Dumb Bunnies headed back to town.

On their way, they came across the deal of the century!

"Duh, look!" said Poppa Bunny. "A free car! Let's take it!"

THE GAS STATION
"We've GoT Gas!"
SORRY, We're OPEN
FREE CAR WASH

So they did.

When the Dumb Bunnies got to town, they parked their new car and went to see a movie.

Inside the lobby, they bought a tub of popcorn.

But the Dumb Bunnies didn't enjoy the movie very much.

"The screen is too small," said Poppa Bunny.
"And it's too *bright*," said Momma Bunny.

After the movie, the Dumb Bunnies could hardly see a thing.

They looked all over for their new car.

"Duh, I think I found it," said Poppa Bunny. So they all climbed in and drove toward home.

It was a very bumpy ride.

CRUNCH
Y-ME

At last, the Dumb Bunnies arrived home safe and sound.

"Dokey-Okey," said Momma and Poppa Bunny.

So Baby Bunny put the TV in his pajamas and watched it all night long.

"That's my boy," said Poppa Bunny.